THE CHRISTMAS DONKEY

By T. William Taylor • Illustrated by Andrea Brooks

A GOLDEN BOOK • NEW YORK
Western Publishing Company, Inc., Racine, Wisconsin

Library of Congress Catalog Card Number: 83-82200
ISBN 0-307-04600-1/ISBN 0-307-60242-7 (lib. bdg.)   G H I J

Many years ago there was a Hebrew farmer who lived in Egypt. Thick green grass grew over the hills of his farm, down the valleys, and all around his house and barn.

The farmer raised donkeys and camels, who ate the grass and grew big and strong. He sold these fine animals to caravan owners, who loaded goods on their backs to be carried to faraway cities.

At sundown each day, when the camels and donkeys came to the watering trough for their evening drink, one little donkey always came by himself. He took a path between two hills, separate from all the other animals.

The farmer loved all his animals, but he loved this small, shaggy donkey best. One evening he said, "Little one, you should have a special name. Since you always take your own path home, I will call you Madrikh. In the language of my people, Madrikh means 'pathfinder.'"

One day a big, gruff man named Rorka came to
the farm. He bought two camels and two donkeys for
his caravan. As he was paying the farmer, he noticed
Madrikh. "That little donkey looks perky," he said.
"How much do you want for him?"

The farmer did not want to sell Madrikh. So he
set a very high price. "Eighteen pieces of silver,"
he said.

To his dismay, Rorka paid in full.

The next morning Rorka's servants piled heavy loads on all the animals except Madrikh. He was so young and small that they did not want to hurt him. But Rorka shouted, "I paid good money for that one. Load him up like all the others!"

Madrikh struggled with his burden, but he was determined to please his new owner.

They traveled all day, around a marshy sea and into the land of Palestine. Madrikh was tired, but he walked on and on.

When the caravan came to a place where five roads met, Rorka stopped at last to eat and sleep. The animals lay down too, but no one took the heavy packs from their backs.

The next day the caravan went on, through
Bethlehem and Jerusalem. Madrikh's legs and back
hurt, and he felt faint. Yet he staggered on.

On the third day, in the town of Nazareth, the aching and weary Madrikh fell down. Rorka whipped him, yelling, "I paid eighteen pieces of silver for you! Get up and work!" The donkey trembled and tried to stand, but he could not.

Rorka picked up a stick to beat Madrikh. But a carpenter who had been watching grabbed his arm. "Do not hit the donkey again," he pleaded. "Can't you see he is tired and hurt?"

"The animal belongs to me," said Rorka. "I'll do what I want with him."

"Then let me buy him from you," said the carpenter.

"All right," said Rorka. "He is no good to me anyway. You can have him—for twenty-five pieces of silver."

The carpenter counted his coins. "Would you sell him for twenty-four?" he asked. "That's all I have."

Rorka grabbed the money. "Madrikh is yours," he snarled.

The carpenter gave the donkey cool water to drink and gently washed the dust from his face.

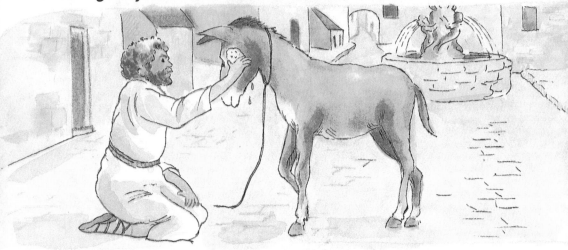

He led Madrikh to a small house at the edge of town. At the gate he called, "Mary! Come see what I've brought you."

A beautiful young woman came to the door. "A donkey!" she exclaimed. "Oh, Joseph, what a wonderful gift!"

How Mary and Joseph loved Madrikh! They fed
him well and tended his wounds. In a few weeks he
was fat and happy and healthy again.

One day a man came to speak to Joseph. Madrikh heard him say, "You must go to Bethlehem, where you were born, to pay your taxes."

"But my wife is about to have a baby," said Joseph. "I must stay with her."

"The law says you must go," said the man, and he left.

Joseph turned to Madrikh. "You will have to help us tomorrow," he said.

Madrikh rubbed his head against Joseph's arm. He was happy to be able to do something for his new owners.

Their journey was long. By the time they reached Bethlehem all the inns were full. There was no place to stay.

One innkeeper took pity on them. "There is some room in my stable," he said. "You may stay there if you wish."

Late that night Madrikh woke up. He thought he heard singing, and the light from a very bright star was shining through a tiny window. Then he heard the soft cry of a baby. He looked into the next stall and saw a glorious sight: Mary was holding a new baby boy.

Madrikh was so proud! He knew the baby was a member of his family and so belonged to him too.

Soon people began coming to see the baby. Some were saying, "Perhaps he is the king, the Messiah." Madrikh didn't know what that meant, but he could see that everyone loved the baby, and that made him glad.

A few days later three kings came with gifts for the baby. Madrikh watched happily as they knelt and worshiped him.

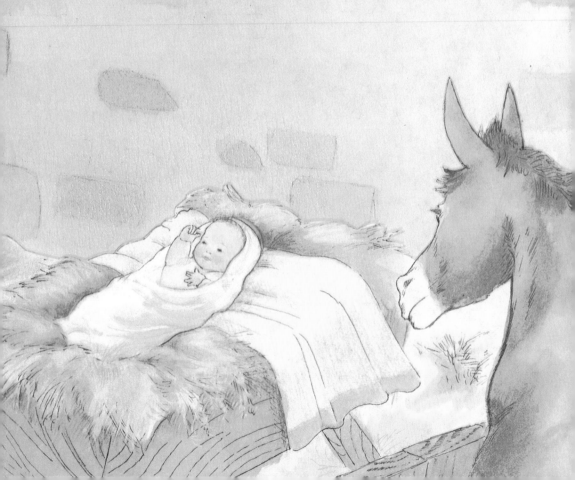

That night Joseph awoke suddenly. "Mary!"
he shouted. "Get up! An angel of God came to me in
a dream. He warned me that King Herod is sending
soldiers to kill the baby Jesus. We must all flee!"

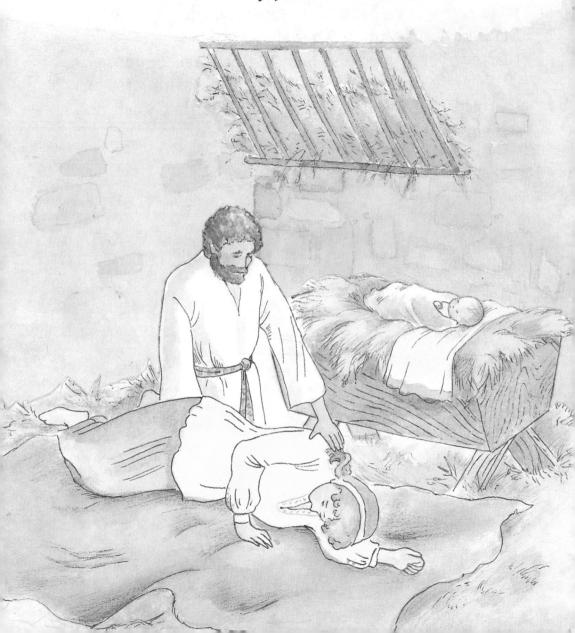

They hurried along the road out of Bethlehem. But when they came to a place where five roads met, Joseph stopped. "I don't know where the soldiers will come from," he cried. "Oh, God, which way shall we go?"

Madrikh perked his ears up. His nostrils quivered. *He* knew which way to go. He remembered these five roads! He ran down one of them as fast as he could. Joseph could barely keep up.

On and on they went. The next day they traveled around a marshy sea and into the land of Egypt. At last they came to a group of hills. Below them was a farm where thick green grass grew all around. Madrikh trotted down a path between two hills, straight to a watering trough.

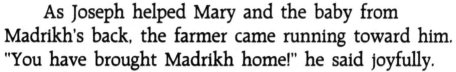

As Joseph helped Mary and the baby from Madrikh's back, the farmer came running toward him. "You have brought Madrikh home!" he said joyfully.

"No," said Joseph. "Madrikh brought us here. We had to leave Palestine because our child's life was in danger. We did not know where to go."

The man looked at Joseph and his family. Then he smiled. "Please stay here with me," he said. "Madrikh has found the path home. If he brought you, it must be God's will."